Sea Snaps

Diana Noonan

Hi, I'm Helen.
I take photos of plants and animals.

Today, I will take photos under the sea.
There are lots of plants and animals down there.
Come and see!

Under the sea, there is a garden of seaweed. Some seaweed is green, some is pink, and some is brown.

This is a seahorse.
The seahorse lives in the seaweed.

This seahorse holds on to the seaweed with its tail.

This is an anemone (say *ah-nem-o-nee.*) It looks like a flower, but it is an animal.

An anemone has wiggly arms.
Its arms sting little animals that swim past.

The wiggly arms push food into the anemone's mouth.

This is a sea urchin.
It looks like a plant, but it is an animal, too!

A sea urchin has lots of spines.
But some animals can still eat it!

These rocks look dark and dull, but there are lots of animals in them!

Here is an octopus.

Here is an eel hiding in some rocks.

The animals hide in the rocks. When fish swim past, they come out and grab them!

Lots of animals live on the seabed.
Crabs live on the seabed.

This is a hermit crab.
It carries a shell on its back.

Lobsters live on the seabed, too.
Lobsters and crabs have hard shells.

Here is an old ship!
It must have sunk
a long time ago.

Look out! **SHARKS!**

Time to go!

Index